This book belongs to

..........................................

..........................................

# Meet the Large family

## Mr Large

Mr Large does his best to help out around the house and manages to stay calm amid the chaos created by his boisterous children.

## Lester Large

Nine-year-old Lester just wants to look cool and play on his skateboard. He loves his family, but often finds them a bit embarrassing.

## Luke Large

Luke is cheerful and sometimes shy. He looks up to his cool older brother Lester, but still enjoys playing with his toys, especially his old favourite, Mr Teddy.

## Mrs Large

Mrs Large is always in a rush as she struggles to cope with her four children and mountains of washing. But she always has time to join in the fun!

## Laura Large

Helpful and good-natured, Laura is a caring big sister to baby Lucy. She is creative and practical and enjoys making things.

## Lucy Large

Lucy is the baby of the family. She gets into mischief the moment Mrs Large turns her back and her naughty little trunk finds its way into everything.

First published 2008 by Walker Books Ltd
87 Vauxhall Walk, London SE11 5HJ

2 4 6 8 10 9 7 5 3 1

This book has been typeset in Bembo Educational.

Printed in China

British Library Cataloguing in Publication Data: a catalogue record for this book
is available from the British Library

ISBN 978-1-40631475-5

www.walkerbooks.co.uk

# Lester Learns
# a Lesson

Based on the Large Family stories by Jill Murphy

# WALKER BOOKS
### AND SUBSIDIARIES
LONDON · BOSTON · SYDNEY · AUCKLAND

Luke and Mrs Large arrived back from shopping, to find Lester sitting on the ground next to his skateboard. Luke peered at his brother through a magnifying glass.

"*I'd* say that Lester has fallen off his skateboard!" he announced.

"No, I haven't," said Lester, crossly. "I was just having a little rest. Anyway, Luke, what's with the weird outfit?"

"It's my new detective set," replied Luke.

"Has anyone got any mysteries for me to solve?" Luke asked.

"Well," said Laura, "I've lost a paintbrush. You can look for that if you like."

Luke jumped up and grabbed his magnifying glass. "I'm on the case!" he replied.

"No skateboards in the kitchen," said Mrs Large,
as Lester nearly ran Luke over.
"It's not fair," grumbled Lester. "I'm not allowed
to skate *anywhere*."

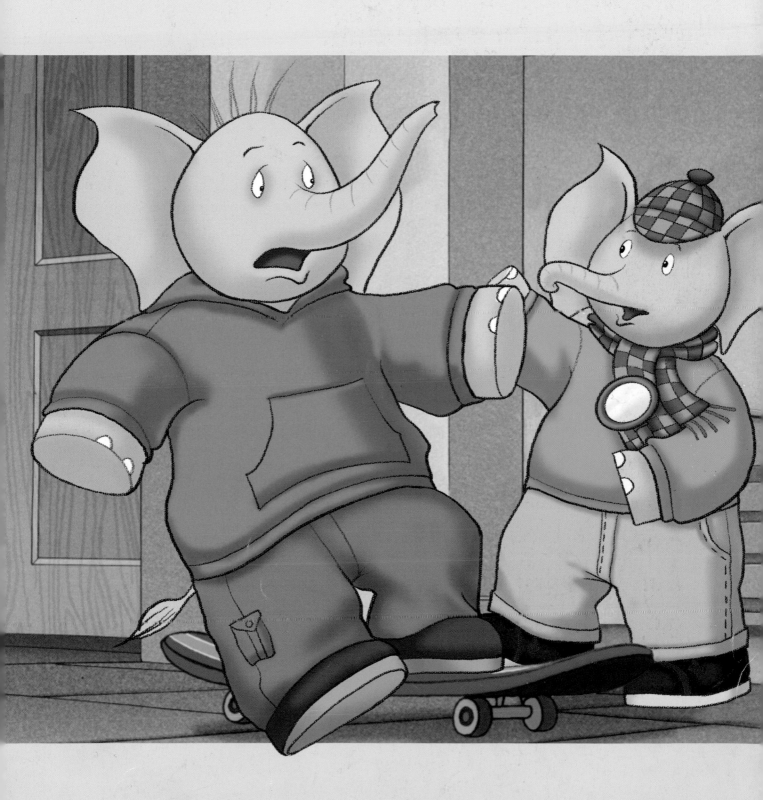

In the bathroom, Luke found some clues to the mystery of the missing paintbrush. He soon discovered it in the bath, and proudly took it downstairs to Laura.

"I've solved the mystery!" he called. "And I can tell you who had the paintbrush. It was Lucy!"
"You don't have to be a detective to work *that* one out!" laughed Lester.

"Now then," said Mrs Large, "who wants to help me with a *really* fun job?"
"I do!" yelled Laura and Luke at the same time.
"Excellent!" said Mrs Large. "We're off to clean the car then. Lester, you can keep an eye on the baby."

Lester decided to cheer himself up by showing
Lucy some of his skateboarding tricks
in the kitchen.

Suddenly the skateboard flipped into the air.
It hit Mrs Large's pink elephant ornament,
which fell off the shelf and smashed to pieces.
Lucy laughed and clapped her hands.

"It's not funny, Lucy!" groaned Lester. "Mum'll go mad when she finds out."
He quickly wrapped the broken elephant in a newspaper and hid it upstairs.

"I think there's something missing," said
Mrs Large, gazing along the shelves
during lunch.
"Yes, dear," replied Mr Large. "It's my
newspaper. I can't find it anywhere."

"*I* know, Mum!" exclaimed Laura. "It's your pink elephant."

"So it is!" agreed Mrs Large. "I wonder what's happened to it?"

"Sounds like a job for a *detective*!" declared Luke, dashing off to begin the hunt.

Laura spotted Lester looking guilty. "If *I* was a detective," she said, "*I'd* say you were up to no good, Lester."

"You're right, Laura," whispered Lester. "I broke Mum's elephant. It was an accident. Do you think I could buy another one just like it?"

"Impossible!" said Laura. "Mum's auntie made it ages ago."

"Do you think you could help me make another one out of your modelling clay?" grovelled Lester. "*Please*, Laura. You're so brilliant at making things."

"Well," said Laura, "I suppose we could give it a try."

Luke was still on the hunt for the missing elephant when he overheard Lester and Laura talking in Laura's bedroom.

"I don't think you've made that trunk big enough," said Lester.
"Yes, I have," said Laura. "Anyway, once we've painted it pink, Mum'll never know the difference!"

Luke raced downstairs to tell Mrs Large that he had solved the mystery of her missing ornament.

"I've put all the clues together," he said, importantly, "and now I can tell you that your elephant has been broken by none other than Laura Large!"

"*Laura!?*" exclaimed Mrs Large. "Are you sure?"

"Absolutely," said Luke. "She's made a new one and she's going to paint it pink, so you won't know the difference – shall we call the police?"

"I don't think so, dear," replied Mrs Large with a smile. "I'm sure I can handle it."

Mrs Large summoned Laura. "Luke has been investigating," she said, "and he thinks that you broke my missing elephant." "*Me?*" exclaimed Laura.

Lester came into the room. "It wasn't Laura.
It was me," he confessed. "I'm so sorry, Mum.
I was skateboarding and I knocked it off
the shelf."
"Well, I'm glad you owned up," said
Mrs Large, "– even if it did take you
some time."

"Laura helped me make a new one,"
said Lester. "It's not very good, I'm afraid,
but you can have it anyway, Mum."

"Thank you," said Mrs Large. "I have to say, it's much nicer than the other one! I'll put it right next to my favourite vase. Now, if you'd broken *that*…"

At that very moment, Lucy stepped onto the skateboard and fell against the dresser. The vase wobbled backwards and forwards, then toppled off the shelf!

Lester dived across the kitchen and caught
it just before it hit the ground.
"Howzat!" he yelled, and everyone burst
out laughing.

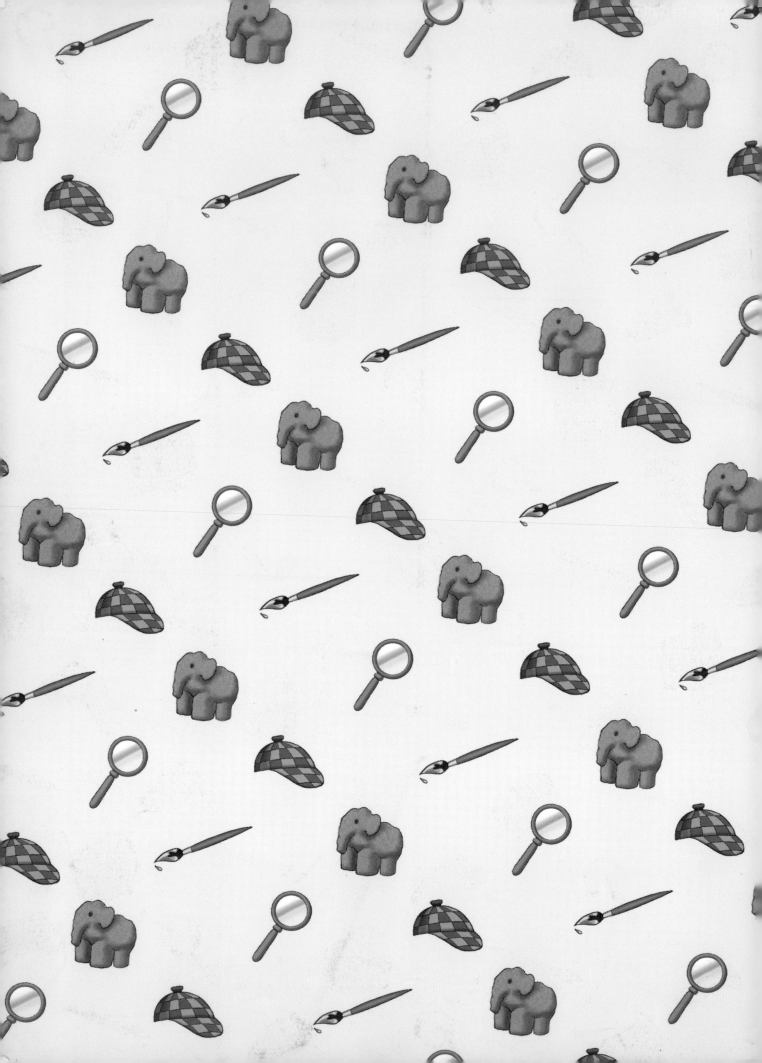